PROLOGUE:
POSEIDON AND THE SEA OF FURY
I AM *PYTHIA,* THE *ORACLE OF DELPHI,* IN GREECE.
I HAVE THE POWER TO *SEE* THE FUTURE.
HEAR MY *PROPHECY:* I SEE DANCERS LURKING AHEAD.
WAIT—MAKE THAT *DANGER* LURKING!
THE FUTURE CAN BE BLURRY, ESPECIALLY WHEN MY EYEGLASSES ARE FOGGY.
ANYHOO, *BEWARE!*

TITAN GIANTS NOW RULE ALL OF EARTH'S DOMAINS...
...OCEANS, MOUNTAINS, FORESTS...
...AND THE DEPTHS OF THE UNDERWEAR.
CRUSH THEM!
EAT THEM!
DESTROY THEM!
STOMP
STOMP
STOMP
FLEE!

OOPS, MAKE THAT UNDERWORLD.
LED BY KING CRONUS...
...THE TITAN GIANTS SEEK TO DESTROY US ALL!
ROARRRRR!
WE ARE DOOMED!

AND YET, I FORESEE HOPE.
A BAND OF RIGHTFUL RULERS CALLED OLYMPIANS WILL RISE.
THOUGH THEIR SIZE AND YOUTH ARE NO MATCH FOR THE TITANS, THEY WILL BE GIANT IN HEART, MIND, AND SPIRIT.
ONE WHO IS DESTINED TO BECOME KING OF THE GODS AND RULER OF THE HEAVENS.
IF HE IS BRAVE ENOUGH.
THEY AWAIT THEIR LEADER— A VERY SPECIAL, YET CLUELESS, GODBOY.
AND IF HE ACCEPTS THAT SOMETIMES HE MUST SHARE THE PAGE— UM—STAGE WITH FIENDS.
OOPS, FRIENDS!
FOR ONLY BY WORKING TOGETHER WILL THESE YOUNG RULERS-TO-BE HAVE A CHANCE AT SAVING THE WORLD!

CHAPTER ONE:
UNDER ATTACK!
HALT OR YOU'RE *DEAD MEAT,* SNACKBOY!
WHIZZZZ
HERA! POSEIDON!
RUN!
WHAT DO YOU *THINK* WE'RE DOING?
YUP! YUP!
THUNNK!

ZEUS RECOGNIZES THE *VOICES*—KING CRONUS'S *LACKEYS,* THOSE HUNGRY HALF-GIANTS THAT ZEUS NICKNAMED!
I SAID *HALT!*
WHEN WE CATCH YOU, WE *WILL* EAT YOU!
HA-HA-HA! YEAH...
DOUBLE CHIN!
BLACKBEARD!
LION TATTOO!
...AND WE'LL CHOMP YOUR *FRIENDS* FOR *DESSERT!*
NEITHER OF THOSE THINGS SOUND LIKE A GOOD REASON TO HALT!
STOMP STOMP STOMP
DO SOMETHING, THUNDERBOY!

ZEUS LIKES IT WHEN HERA CALLS HIM "THUNDERBOY"...
SO CLOSE!
WHOOOOSH
WHOA!
OKAY– DIVE!
...TOO BAD SHE ALWAYS SOUNDS MAD WHEN SHE SAYS IT!
OUCH!
OWW!
THOK
WUSS.
BUMMP
THUMP
I'M NOT A WUSS. I'M AN OLYMPIAN!
I'M AN OLYMPIAN TOO.
AND YOU DON'T HEAR ME WHINING!
CAN YOU BOTH STOP ARGUING FOR HALF A SECOND?
THOSE CRONIES ARE GOING TO HEAR YOU!
UNNGH
HOW DO THEY HEAR ANYTHING OVER THEIR OWN FOOTSTEPS?
DO YOU REALLY THINK THEY'LL EAT US?
THEY'LL MORE LIKELY DRAG US BACK FOR KING CRONUS TO SWALLOW US WHOLE!
NOW BE QUIET!

THEIR STOMPING HAS FADED OFF.
THINK WE LOST THEM?
THE COAST LOOKS CLEAR.
SO, WHAT NOW?
LET'S FIND OUT.
ALL RIGHT, CHIP...
...WHICH WAY?
OKAY, THEN...

...THAT WAY!
MORE WALKING?
MY FEET ARE KILLING ME!

MINE ARE AS WELL.
BUT IT'S GOT TO BE WORSE FOR YOU.
I'M BETTING YOU DIDN'T WALK ANY GREAT DISTANCES, LIVING INSIDE THE BELLY OF A GIANT YOUR WHOLE LIFE.

WE'VE JOURNEYED OVER HILLS, ACROSS VALLEYS, THROUGH FORESTS–
YEAH...

...WHILE YOU WERE WUSSING THE WHOLE WAY!

WHOOOSH
HEY!
DOWN, BOY!
SKRASSH!
THEY'RE BAAACK!
FEE, FI, FO, FUM!
LOOK OUT, SNACKLETS!
HERE WE COME!
STOMP! STOMP! STOMP!

SPEED IT UP!
I THOUGHT YOUR FEET HURT!
DYING BY ARROW WOULD HURT WORSE!
HA-HA-HA
STOMP STOMP STOMP STOMP
CAW! CAW! CAW!
WE MUST BE GETTING CLOSE TO THE SEA NOW!
YOU'RE RIGHT. LOOK!

TROUBLE, TROUBLE, BOIL AND BUBBLE!
YOU MUST FIND THE ***TRIDENT***— ONE THAT WILL POINT THE WAY TO THOSE YOU SEEK.
ONE THAT, IN THE RIGHT HANDS, HAS THE POWER TO ***DEFEAT*** THE FIRST OF THE KING'S ***CREATURES OF CHAOS!***
THE ORACLE WAS RIGHT!
THE ***SEA***— IT'S ***BOILING!***
REMEMBER WHAT SHE ***SAID!***
WE'VE GOT TO FIND THAT ***TRIDENT*** BEFORE SOMEONE ELSE DOES!
I DON'T EVEN KNOW WHAT A TRIDENT IS!
STOMP STOMP

THEY'RE SO CLOSE, I CAN SMELL THEM!
STOMP

THWIPPP
THE HALF-GIANTS WILL BE ON TOP OF US IN SECONDS!
YEOW!
THWUNK
WE'RE ON A QUEST. I NEVER EXPECTED IT TO BE FAST OR EASY.
A PAINFUL REMINDER...
OWW!
ZZZZZT
...THAT HE HAS A WEAPON TO FIGHT BACK WITH!
YOU GUYS KEEP RUNNING...
STOMP
STOMP
STOMP
...I'LL CATCH UP WITH YOU!
OKAY!

BOLT... LARGE!
STOMP
STOMP
STOMP
KRK
KRK•
KRK•
OOOOMPH! ZAP THEM, BOLT!
ZIPPPP!
BZZZT•
KRA•KLE
GET 'EM!
ATTABOY!
WAIT... ...WHAT?

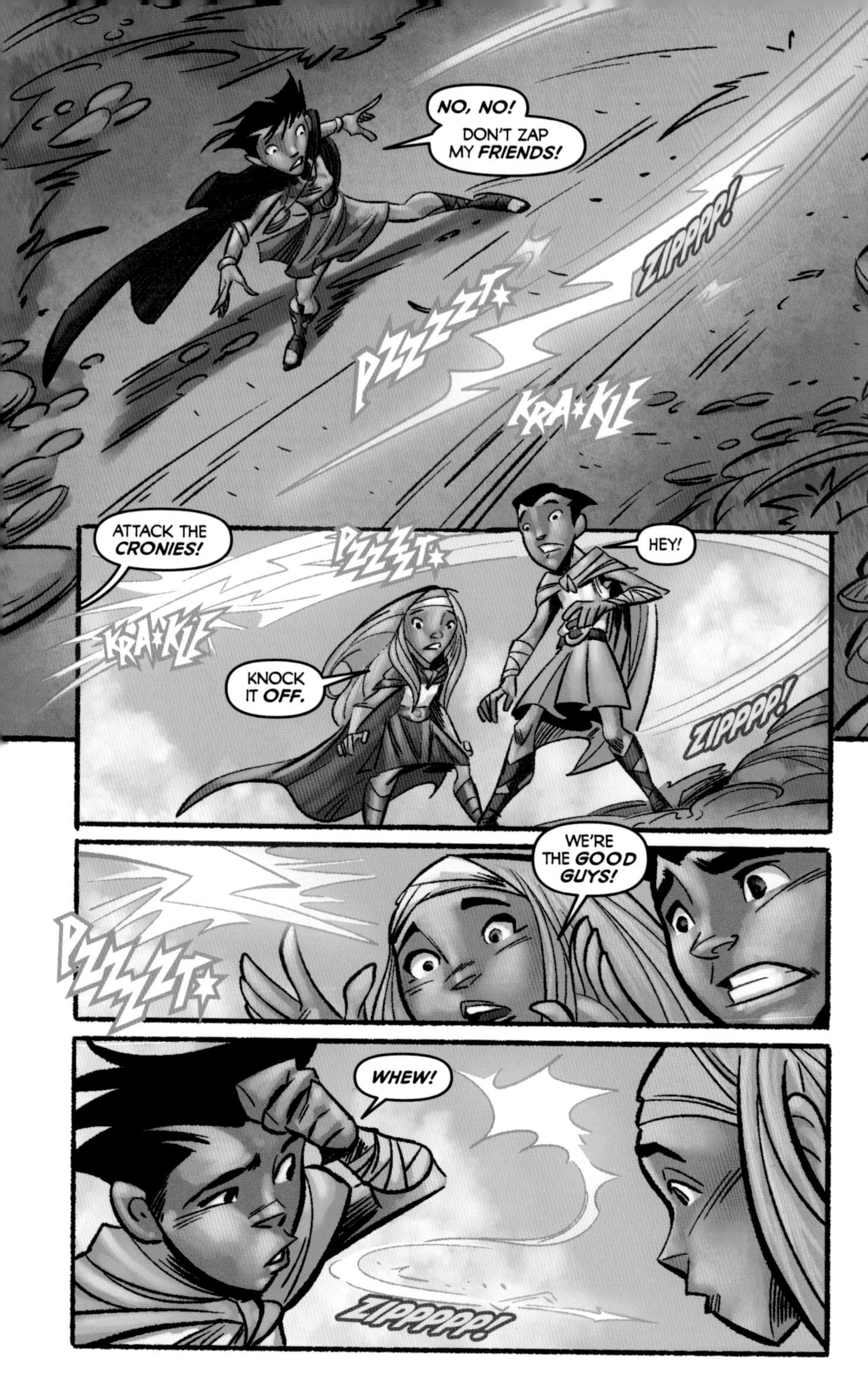
NO, NO!
DON'T ZAP MY FRIENDS!
ZIPPPP!
PZZZZZT*
KRA*KLE
ATTACK THE CRONIES!
PZZZZT*
HEY!
KRA*KLE
KNOCK IT OFF.
ZIPPPP!
WE'RE THE GOOD GUYS!
PZZZZT*
WHEW!
ZIPPPPP!

ARE YOU BOTH OKAY?
WATCH HOW YOU THROW THAT THING, THUNDERBOY!
YOU NEED TO BE REALLY SPECIFIC WITH YOUR COMMANDS.
OH NO, NO, NO!
STOMP
STOMP
STOMP
OWWW!
ATTACK!
WHOOOOSH!
ZIP!
BRZAPPP!
FIZZZT!
ZIP!
KRA•KLE

OOOOF!
BRA-KOOOOOM!
ZIPPPP
YARRGH!
WHUMMP!
ZIP!
OUCH! OUCH!
PZZZT
PZZZZT
EEEP! OWWW!
ZIP!
PZZZT
ZIP!
RETREAT!
PZZZZT
KRAK-KRAK-KRACKLE
OW! OW!
WHOOOOSH
ZIP!
ZIP!
ZIP!

CHAPTER TWO:
SEA JOURNEY
ZIPPPPPP
KRA*KLE
GOOD BOY, BOLT!
WHY IS THE SEA BOILING?
ARE THOSE CRONIES GONE?
PLUNNK!
ZEUS BEGINS TO APPRECIATE WHAT BOLT HAS TO OFFER THEIR QUEST.

GONE FOR NOW, ANYWAY...
...BUT MORE WILL COME.
SMALL, BOLT!
KRK*
KRK
KRK*
THEN LET'S GET OUT OF HERE.
ANY FRESH IDEA ABOUT WHERE TO LOOK FOR THAT "TRIDENT" THING?
UMMMM... MAYBE.
CHECK THIS OUT.
UMM-
WAIT, WAIT, WAIT, WAIT, WAIT!
THE SEA? WE'RE SUPPOSED TO DIVE INTO A SCALDING-HOT SEA AND STEW OURSELVES TO DEATH?
I CAN'T SWIM!
AND IF ANY OF US FALL INTO THAT SEAWATER, WE'LL MELT!
BOILED ALIVE IS MORE LIKE IT.
I KNOW WE HAVE TO GO, BUT HE DOES HAVE A POINT.
WUSS.

HIP-SIP.
HIP-SIP.
DID YOUR AMULET JUST TALK?
UM, YEAH. GUESS I FORGOT TO TELL YOU IT DOES THAT.
WHAT DOES "HIP-SIP" MEAN?
I CALL IT CHIP LATIN. SORT OF LIKE PIG LATIN.
YOU MOVE THE FIRST LETTER OF A WORD TO THE END AND ADD AN "IP" SOUND.
AS IN "CHIP."
SO "HIP-SIP" MEANS "SHIP"!
WHERE CAN WE GET A SHIP?
GUESS WE'RE SUPPOSED TO FIGURE OUT THAT PART ON OUR OWN.
OH...

WELL, THEN... I–
HERA, WHAT ARE YOU DOING?
UNHHH
SIGH I'M TRYING TO USE SOME MAGIC POWERS TO GET US A SHIP!
WAIT, YOU HAVE MAGIC POWERS...?
LOOK, IF YOU CAN COMMAND A MAGIC THUNDERBOLT...
...IT MUST MEAN THAT POSEIDON AND I CAN DO MAGIC TOO.
AFTER ALL, WE'RE ALL OL–
JUST STOP.
OWW!
HUH?
...
NOTHING.
FORGET IT.
WE'RE ALL WHAT?

"THE OTHERS."
HERA AND I DON'T KNOW FOR SURE THAT WE HAVE MAGIC POWERS.
ALL WE ***DO*** KNOW IS THAT KING CRONUS ***FEARS*** US– AND THE OTHERS.
YOU MEAN YOUR FRIENDS WHO ESCAPED CRONUS'S BELLY...
...AND YOU WANT ME TO HELP ***FIND*** THEM?
YES. THEY'RE ***OLYMPIANS*** LIKE US...
...WHATEVER THAT MEANS...
...AND WERE IMPRISONED IN THERE FOR ***YEARS!***
CRONUS MAY FEAR YOU–
BUT I THINK HE FEARS ***ME,*** TOO.
JUST WISH I KNEW ***WHY.***
UMMM...
EXCUSE ME...
...ARE YOU LOOKING FOR ***TRANSPORT?***

YES, SIR.
WE ARE.
FOLLOW ME.
A SMALL BOAT WASHED UP THIS MORNING THAT NOBODY HAS CLAIMED.
YOU'RE WELCOME TO IT.
WHERE ARE ALL THE OTHER BOATS?
AND ALL THE FISHERMEN?
MISSY, THERE ARE NO MORE FISHERMEN ON THIS SEA.
NOT SINCE THE WATER BEGAN TO BOIL.
WILL OF THE GODS, SOME SAY.
IT KILLED THE FISH, ALONG WITH ANY SEAMAN UNLUCKY ENOUGH TO FALL IN.
OUR ONE INDUSTRY WAS MAKING FISHNETS– EASILY THE STRONGEST NET IN THE WORLD.
FASHIONED FROM A RECIPE FROM THE GODS, THEY SAY.
EVEN THAT BUSINESS IS GONE NOW.
MOST FOLKS SEEM TO HAVE LEFT THESE PARTS...
...BUT A FEW SCAVENGE FRESHLY DEAD FISH THAT FLOAT UP FROM SOME COLDER-WATER FISSURE.
SOME ARE STILL GOOD EATIN'.

LOOK AT THE NAME PAINTED ON ITS SIDE!
THERE'S NO WAY I'M GETTING INTO A BOAT NAMED SINKER!
LOOK CLOSER. THERE'S A T FADED OUT.
SO IT'S NOT NAMED "SINKER."
IT'S–
"STINKER"? OH, SOOO MUCH BETTER!
STINKER
I'M NOT YOUR GUARDIAN, BUT ANY PARENT WOULD WARN YOU NOT TO GO OUT IN THESE ROUGH SEAS.
YOU'D BE CRAZY TO. NEVER SEEN THEM THIS ANGRY!
ONE CHURNING, BOILING WAVE COULD END A LIFE!

WE APPRECIATE THAT, SIR, BUT I'M AFRAID WE MUST.
WE'RE ON A BIT OF A QUEST!
A QUEST, EH?
THEN IT SEEMS TO ME YOU'VE NO CHOICE BUT TO SAIL A FURIOUS SEA!
HELP ME PUSH!
SURE. UNNGH!
THANK YOU FOR YOUR WISDOM AND KINDNESS, SIR!
NKER
GOOD LUCK TO YOU ALL...
...AND GODS SPEED!

CHAPTER THREE:
FIIISSSHH
ANYONE KNOW HOW TO STEER A *BOAT?*
EEEP.
I'M SURE I CAN FIGURE IT OUT.
I MEAN, HOW *HARD* CAN IT *BE?*
TOO LATE, ZEUS REALIZES THAT HE SHOULD HAVE ASKED THAT KINDLY OLD FISHERMAN TO *TEACH* THEM A THING OR TWO.

CRASSHHH

SHE'LL BE BOILED ALIVE!
OH NO!
STINKER
YIKES!

OHHHH!
SPLASH!
HERA!
HERA!
OH NONONONONO...
PULL ME UP!
GASP!
SPLISHH

COUGH COUGH
HOW BADLY ARE YOU BURNED?
HOW ARE YOU EVEN ALIVE?
IT'S WEIRD. THE WATER DIDN'T FEEL THAT HOT TO ME...
...EVEN THOUGH IT'S BOILING!
REALLY? THAT'S... STRANGE!
I WONDER...
NO, POSEIDON, WAIT!
YOU'RE RIGHT!
EVEN THE VILE LIQUIDS IN KING CRONUS'S STOMACH WERE HOTTER THAN THIS.

MAYBE ITS *FURY* IS JUST MEANT TO SCARE PEOPLE *AWAY* FROM THE SEA...
...SO THEY WON'T GO SEARCHING FOR THE *TRIDENT.*
OR MAYBE IT'S BECAUSE WE ARE *OLYMPIANS,* AND WE CAN'T BE HURT BY HOT WATER.
I MEAN, WE DID LIVE FOR TEN YEARS INSIDE A GIANT'S *BELLY!*
WHILE YOU TWO *GENIUSES* PUZZLE OVER IT...
...I'VE FIGURED OUT HOW TO *STEER* THIS THING!
I JUST MOVE THIS IN THE DIRECTION *OPPOSITE* OF WHERE WE WANT TO GO.
SO WHERE *DO* WE WANT TO GO?
ANYWHERE BUT HERE...

...BECAUSE I FEEL SEASICK.
BLAHHHHH!
HANG YOUR HEAD OVER THE SIDE— NOW!
BLORRCH!
BLERRRT!
WHEW! OH, WOW.
I FEEL BETTER NOW.
IN FACT, I'M HUNGRY.

OKAY, HE'S RIGHT. WE *SHOULD* EAT.

MAYBE SOME FISH ARE STILL ALIVE IN THIS WATER.

MAYBE YOU COULD SPEAR ONE WITH YOUR *THUNDERBOLT!*

ARE YOU *KIDDING?*

IF THIS THUNDERBOLT GETS *WET*...

...IT COULD ELECTROCUTE US *ALL!*

HERA'S SMART ABOUT *SOME* THINGS, ZEUS THINKS, BUT SHE OBVIOUSLY DOESN'T KNOW THAT LIGHTNING AND WATER DON'T MIX.

MMMM... FIIISSSHH.
I WISH I COULD CATCH ONE RIGHT *NOW!*
SPLASH!
FIDDLING *FISH CAKES!*
WHOA!
THUMMP!
HOW?

HELP.
HELP!
HELP!
HELP!
GOT YOU!
THAT WAS CLOSE!
I'LL SAY!
TOO CLOSE.
SO... ...DINNER?
THANK YOU. BOTH OF YOU.

SO IS CALLING UP DINNER YOUR MAGIC POWER?
THAT COULDN'T HAVE BEEN A COINCIDENCE.
MAYBE YOU CAN TALK TO FISH!
YEAH. MAYBE.

OR MAYBE MY MAGIC POWER IS TO SUMMON ANYTHING WE NEED!
WHY NOT?
TRY IT!

I WISH THE TRIDENT WOULD SHOW UP NOW!
AT LEAST WE HAVE FOOD.
SIGH

LOOKS LIKE THIS FISH DIED IN YOUR ARMS, POSEIDON!
PZZZT
MUST'VE COME UP FROM THE COLDER SEA DEPTHS AND HALF-COOKED AS IT SURFACED!
NOT A NICE WAY TO GO.
HE CAME WHEN YOU WANTED HIM, PAL.
NOW HELP ME HOLD HIM.
PZZZZT
INKER
I'M USING BOLT, NOT ONLY TO REMOVE THE FISH SCALES...
PZZZZT
...BUT ALSO TO SLICE UP PORTIONS.
BOLT DOES A GREAT JOB BROILING THE FISH AS IT CUTS!

YOU MASTERED USING BOLT PRETTY *QUICKLY,* ZEUS.
I'M A BOY OF *MANY* TALENTS!
I'M GLAD THAT BEING A QUICK *COOK* IS ONE OF THEM!
I COULD EAT SEAFOOD *EVERY* DAY OF THE WEEK!
IT'S GOOD, BUT I WOULDN'T EAT IT *EVERY* DAY...
THIS WOULD BE BETTER WITH *SEASONING*...
...BUT I BET IT BEATS *CRONUS*'S LEFTOVERS!
ME, I'M ON A SEAFOOD DIET.
WHEN I SEE FOOD, I *EAT* IT!
STINKER
FOR THE FIRST TIME SINCE MEETING THESE OLYMPIANS, ZEUS FEELS MAYBE THEY COULD BE FRIENDS.

OR MAYBE IT'S JUST THE FEELING OF A FULL BELLY...
THIS WAY.
GOT IT.
...AND BECAUSE NOBODY'S CHASING THEM.
SO TELL ME ABOUT THE OTHER OLYMPIANS YOU WANT MY HELP TO FIND.
HADES. DEMETER. HESTIA.
TWO OTHER GIRLS AND A BOY.
I STILL DON'T UNDERSTAND WHY CRONUS SWALLOWED ALL FIVE OF YOU.

DUH.
TO KEEP US *IMPRISONED.*
BECAUSE HE FEARS SOME MAGIC POWERS YOU *MIGHT* HAVE?
LIKE CALLING FOR FISH TO EAT?
SEEMS AS THOUGH HE'D *LIKE* THAT!
WHY WOULD HE THINK THAT'S *DANGEROUS* TO HIM?
I MEAN, YOU DON'T EVEN KNOW EXACTLY WHAT YOUR POWERS *ARE,* MUCH LESS HOW TO *USE* THEM.
HUH? ALL RIGHT.
SO WHAT'S THE BIG *SECRET?*
OH NO– *HANG ON!*
LOOK!

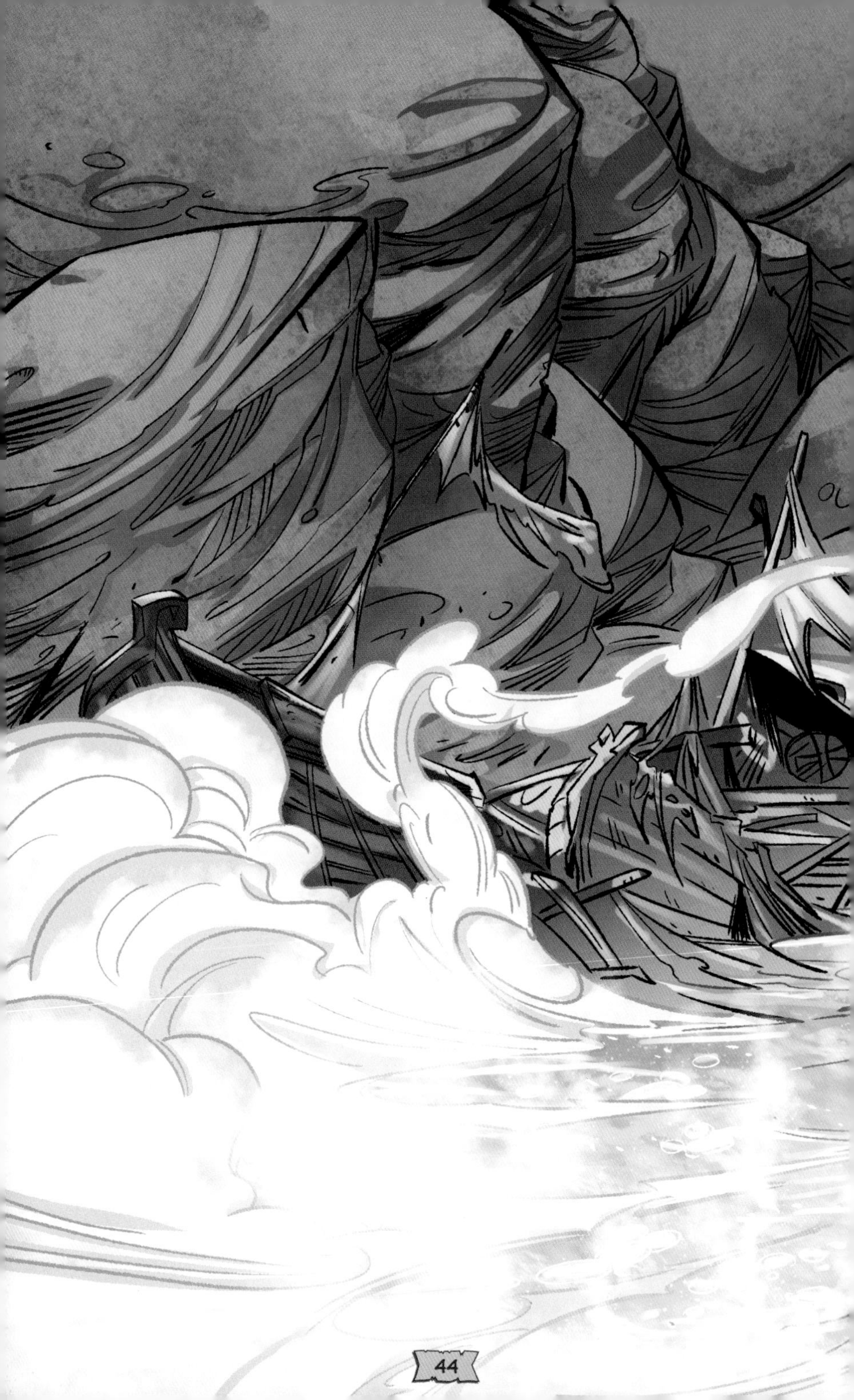

WHAT HAPPENED HERE?
THAT FISHERMAN SAID THAT PEOPLE WENT AWAY WHEN THE WATER STARTED BOILING.
THE SEA'S FURY MUST'VE CAUSED THIS.
OUR BOAT MUST'VE LOST ITS SAILORS AND SOMEHOW AVOIDED THE ROCKS.
I SEE.
THEN THE TIDE WASHED IT ASHORE!

YOU ***LED*** US HERE, ZEUS.

AND FINDING THIS ***BOAT*** WAS MIGHTY CONVENIENT.

HOW DO WE KNOW YOU'RE NOT ONE OF CRONUS'S ***SPIES***...

...AND THIS ISN'T ALL A TRAP FOR US?

THEY CAN'T BE ***SERIOUS!***

HA-HA-HA!

YOU KNOW I HELPED YOU TO ***ESCAPE!***

WHAT ***MORE*** PROOF DO YOU NEED THAT I'M ON ***YOUR*** SIDE?

THE ***TRIDENT.***

YUP.

ARE THEY SERIOUS?

C'MON, I–

SHHHH!

DO YOU HEAR THAT?

HARP MUSIC!
AND BEAUTIFUL SINGING!
ZEUS CAN FEEL THE GLORIOUS SINGING FILLING HIS SOUL!
WHERE IS IT COMING FROM?
OVER THERE!
AND HE REALIZES THAT THE SEARCH FOR THE TRIDENT AND THE OTHER OLYMPIANS ISN'T IMPORTANT AT ALL!
LET'S GO IN FOR A CLOSER LOOK!
OPE-NIP!

TO ZEUS, NOTHING IS MORE IMPORTANT THAN FINDING THE MAKERS OF THE MUSIC!
GREAT IDEA, ZEUS! HURRY!
NO, WAIT!
THE LONGING THAT ZEUS HAS FOR FAMILY BUBBLES UP IN HIM HARDER AND LOUDER THAN THE BOILING SEA.
GOT TO GET CLOSER!
MUST.
LISTEN.
FOREVER.
WHAT'S WRONG WITH THE TWO OF YOU? STOP!

WHY DID HIS PARENTS–
WHOEVER THEY ARE–
ABANDON HIM IN A CAVE?
"WE HAVE ALL THE
ANSWERS," THE WOMEN
SING TO HIM!

ZEUS–
LISTEN!
CHIP IS WARNING US TO TURN AROUND!
CLOSER...

POSEIDON!
SNAP OUT OF IT!
SNAP!
SNAP!

I THINK THOSE WOMEN AND THEIR ROCK MUSIC HAVE PUT YOU BOTH UNDER A MAGIC SPELL!
ONLY, FOR SOME REASON, IT'S NOT AFFECTING ME!

ANGER-DIP!
ANGER-DIP!

THE *MUSIC*... IT HAS TURNED *SINISTER!*

WE'RE GOING TO *CRASH!*

EEEEE-HEEHEE

HEEHEE!

KLONNK
CAN'T WAIT ANY LONGER!
FRUMMP!
OWWW!
OHHH!
GOT! TO! STEER! AWAY!
OH NO-

CHAPTER FOUR:
SEA SERPENTS AND MERPEOPLE
WHAT TH-?
NO!
WHERE DID THEY COME FROM?
SPLOOOOSH

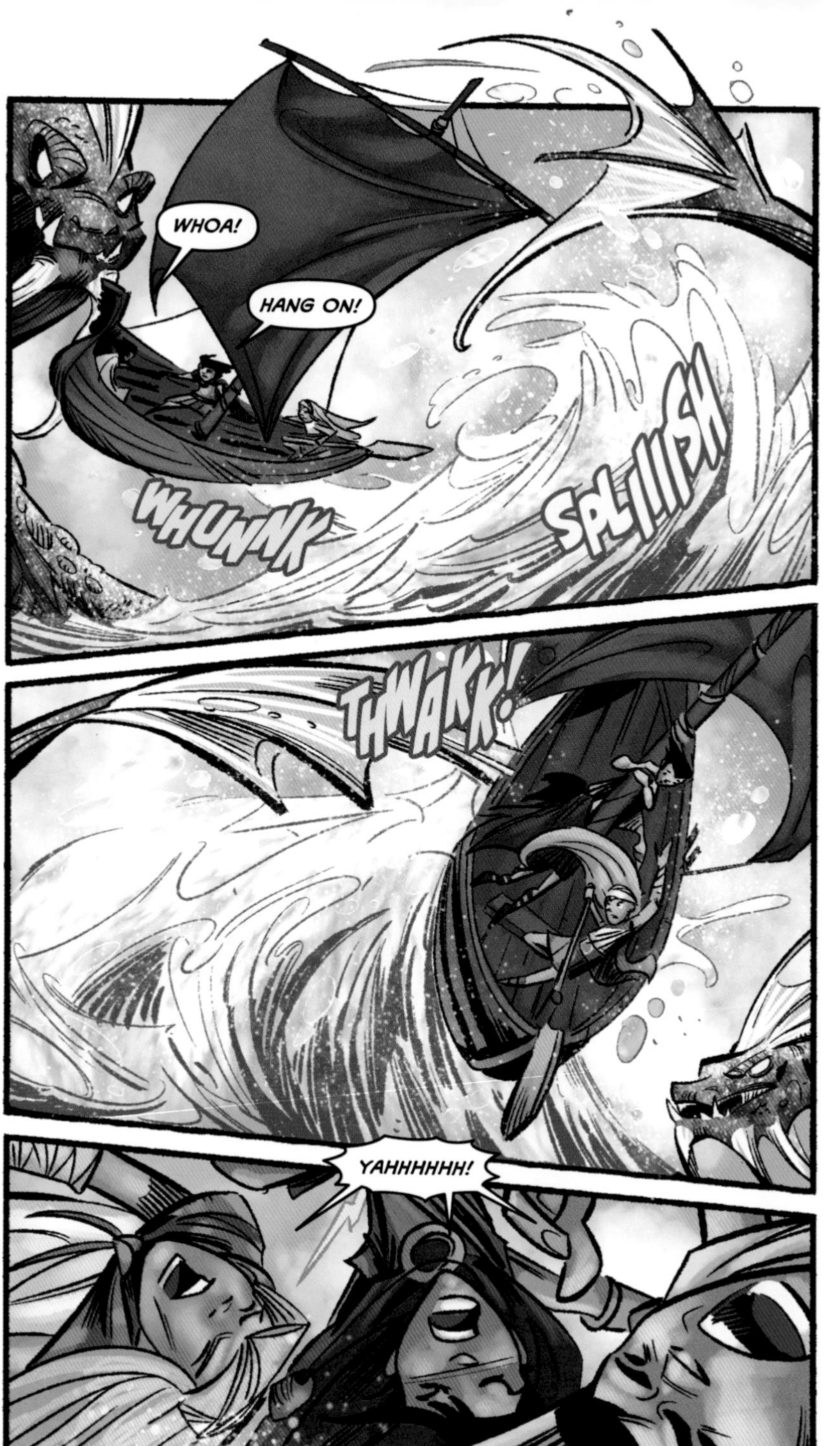

WHOA!
HANG ON!
WHUNNK
SPLIIISH
THWAKK!
YAHHHHHH!

THOKKK
YIYYYYYY!
SPLISSH
SPLOOSSH
SPLASSH

OKAY... *THAT* HURT.

OHHH...

WHAT JUST HAPPENED...?

WHAT'S ***WRONG*** WITH THE TWO OF YOU?

WHY DID YOU LISTEN TO THOSE ***SINGERS?***

UM...

UH, WELL, I–

DON'T BLAME YOURSELVES.

THOSE WERE ***SIRENS.***

YIPE!

GAHHH!

OH!

SPLISH! SPLISH!

THEIR BEAUTIFUL MUSIC LURES SAILORS TO THEIR DEATHS.
MALE SAILORS, THAT IS.
AHA!
WE MAGICAL BEINGS AREN'T BOTHERED BY THE STEAMING SEAS.
BUT HUMANS...
SEE?
THEY PUT US UNDER A CREEPY SPELL.
WHATEVER.
YEAH.
WE COULDN'T HELP IT!
THANKS SO MUCH TO YOU BOTH! WE–
OH. GONE.
SPLOOOOSH
SPLOOOSH
THEY DIDN'T EVEN WAIT FOR A THANK-YOU!

DID YOU SEE HOW THOSE SERPENTS WERE *STARING* AT ME?
IT'S LIKE THEY *KNEW* ME OR SOMETHING!
THAT'S SILLY.
NOBODY HAS *SEEN* US BEFORE.
WE'VE BEEN IN A BIG *BELLY* OUR WHOLE LIVES.
MAYBE.
BUT IT SURE SEEMED TO *ME* THEY WERE STARING EXTRA HARD AT *POSEIDON.*
WAIT— WHERE'S *CHIP?*
ERE-HIP!
HUH?
DON'T *LEAVE* ME LIKE THAT, BUDDY!
ERE-HIP!
WE HAVE A *DIRECTION*...
GOOD.
THE SOONER WE FIND THAT *TRIDENT* THING AND GET *OUT* OF THIS CREEPY SEA, THE BETTER!
YOU BOYS NEED TO LET *ME* STEER!

HERA STEERS, POSEIDON STEERS, ZEUS STEERS–FOR TWO GLOOMY DAYS AND TWO STARLESS NIGHTS.
WHEN IT RAINS, THEY **DRINK.**
WHEN THEY'RE HUNGRY, POSEIDON LOUDLY WISHES FOR FISH.
THEIR **FEET** GET THE REST THEY NEED AND THE BLISTERS QUICKLY HEAL.
THROUGH IT ALL, THEY FOLLOW THE **ARROW** THAT CHIP SHOWS...

...AND THEY TELL THE STORIES OF THEIR *LIVES.*
FLIPPIN' FISH HEADS!
WHO ARE *THEY?*
HUH?
SO IT'S *TRUE.*
THE SEA SERPENTS *TOLD* US YOU WOULD COME ONE DAY.
GIGGLE
WE HAVE WAITED A *LONG TIME* FOR YOU.
GIGGLE
HAVE YOU COME TO RESCUE THE *SEA?*

WHO, *ME...?*
NOT EXACTLY.
WHO ARE *YOU?*
WE'RE *MERPEOPLE.*
WELL, WE'RE HERE TO SEARCH FOR A *TRIDENT.*
HAVE YOU *SEEN* ONE?
SURE!
GOT ONE RIGHT *HERE!*

EVERY MERPERSON HAS ONE!
IS THERE A SPECIAL TRIDENT SOMEWHERE, THOUGH?
A MAGICAL ONE?
OCEANUS HAS THE MIGHTIEST TRIDENT OF THEM ALL.
FEARSOME, WHAT IT CAN DO!
WHERE CAN WE FIND HIM?
FIND HIM?
BAD IDEA.
WHERE ARE YOU FROM?

BELLY.
CAVE.
BELLY.
ULP!
"BELLY"...? INTERESTING!
SPLASH!
SPLOOOSH
HE COULD BE ANYWHERE IN IT.
OCEANUS PRETTY MUCH RULES THE SEA.
IS OCEANUS A FRIEND OF KING CRONUS?
AS MUCH AS ANY OF THE MANY TITANS CAN CONSIDER ANYONE A FRIEND!
MM-HMM.

GASP!
OCEANUS IS A TITAN?
THERE ARE MANY TITANS?
THE NIGHT I THREW BOLT DOWN CRONUS'S THROAT AND RESCUED YOU, ONLY SIX WERE THERE!
SO THERE ARE A LOT OF DARK, HUNGRY STOMACHS?!
OKAY, THUNDERBOY...
...HOW DO WE GET A MAGIC TRIDENT FROM A TITAN?
I DON'T KNOW!
IF WE TOLD HIM PYTHIA WANTS US TO HAVE IT, WOULD HE JUST HAND IT OVER?
NOT A CHANCE!

YOU DON'T FIND HIM.
HE FINDS YOU.
IF YOU ARE VERY, VERY UNLUCKY.
INSTEAD OF LOOKING FOR HIM, YOU SHOULD TURN AROUND...
...AND SAIL AS FAR SOUTH AS POSSIBLE.
BECAUSE THAT'S WHERE HE LIVES?
GIGGLE
GIGGLE
NO.
BECAUSE THAT'S THE BEST WAY TO AVOID BEING BURIED AT SEA!

CHAPTER FIVE:
TRIDENT TROUBLE
"BURIED AT SEA?" HARDLY A PLEASANT THOUGHT.
STILL, GETTING THE TRIDENT IS THE WHOLE POINT OF THEIR QUEST.
THANK YOU ALL!
WE'RE ON IT! GOODBYE!
SWAK
HA! THAT MEANS WE GO NORTH TO FIND OCEANUS, DOOFUS-EIDON!
BUT TITANS ARE MIGHTY BAD NEWS!

HOW CAN WE BE SURE THAT OCEANUS'S TRIDENT IS THE ONE WE'RE AFTER?
YOU HEARD WHAT THE MERPEOPLE SAID: IT'S FEARSOME AND MIGHTY.
HERA, IT MUST BE MAGIC.
PYTHIA DIDN'T ACTUALLY SAY THAT THE TRIDENT IS MAGICAL.
SHE JUST SAID IT WILL POINT THE WAY TO THOSE WE SEEK.
SHE MEANT "TO THE LOST OLYMPIANS"– OUR FRIENDS!
OR–OR– IT COULD POINT TO MY PARENTS!
THAT'S MY HOPE, ANYWAY.
CLUCK CLUCK!
MAYBE ONE TRIDENT IS AS GOOD AS ANOTHER.
PERHAPS ONE OF THOSE MERPEOPLE WOULD LEND US A TRIDENT.
I
AM
NOT!
I THINK SOMEONE'S CHICKENING OUT!

HEY!
TAKE IT BACK!
STOP! SORRY! I'M SORRY!
I TOLD YOU I'LL MELT IF I FALL INTO THE WATER!
ZEUS WONDERS WHY POSEIDON KEEPS SAYING THAT.
REALLY?
ZEUS KNOWS HE HAS SEEN POSEIDON IN WATER BEFORE.
OKAY, SO...
PYTHIA SAID THE TRIDENT HAS THE POWER TO DEFEAT THE FIRST OF THE KING'S CREATURES OF CHAOS.
DON'T YOU THINK A TRIDENT POWERFUL ENOUGH TO DO THAT WOULD HAVE TO BE MAGICAL?
I'D CERTAINLY THINK SO.
MAYBE. BUT...

...THE ORACLE SAID THE TRIDENT HAS POWER ONLY IF IT'S *IN THE RIGHT HANDS.*
WHAT IF *MY* HANDS ARE THE RIGHT ONES?
I SHOULD HAVE THOUGHT OF THIS EARLIER.
OKAY...SO *GO* BACK.
WE WON'T STOP HER, WILL WE?
MAYBE I CAN USE ONE OF THE *MERPEOPLE*'S TRIDENTS TO DEFEAT THOSE *CREATURES OF CHAOS*, WHATEVER THEY ARE.
LOOK, MR. BOSSY *THUNDERPANTS.*
I *DEMAND* THAT YOU TURN THIS BOAT AROUND *NOW*...
IT'S *OCEANUS*'S TRIDENT WE NEED.
I'M ALMOST *SURE* OF IT!

...AND GO FIND THOSE MERPEOPLE AGAIN!
ME, BOSSY? YOU...!
LISTEN...
THE WIND HAS BLOWN US FAR, THEY'RE ALREADY LEFT BEHIND, AND WE'LL LOSE TIME IF WE BACKTRACK NOW!
I SAY WE GO ON.
AND I SAY–
HEY, LOOK! DOLPHINS!
MAYBE YOU SHOULD CATCH A RIDE BACK WITH ONE OF THEM, HERA!
THEN ZEUS AND I COULD HAVE SOME PEACE!
SPLASH
SPLASH

WHAT THE...?
ACK-ACK-ACK-ACK-ACK
DID THAT DOLPHIN *LISTEN* TO ME?
ACK-ACK-ACK-ACK
SEE? THIS PROVES I'M *RIGHT* TO GO BACK.
EVEN THE *DOLPHIN* KNOWS IT!
ACK-ACK-ACK-ACK-ACK
DON'T LOOK AT *ME.*
I'M STAYING *PUT.*
ALL RIGHT, THEN...

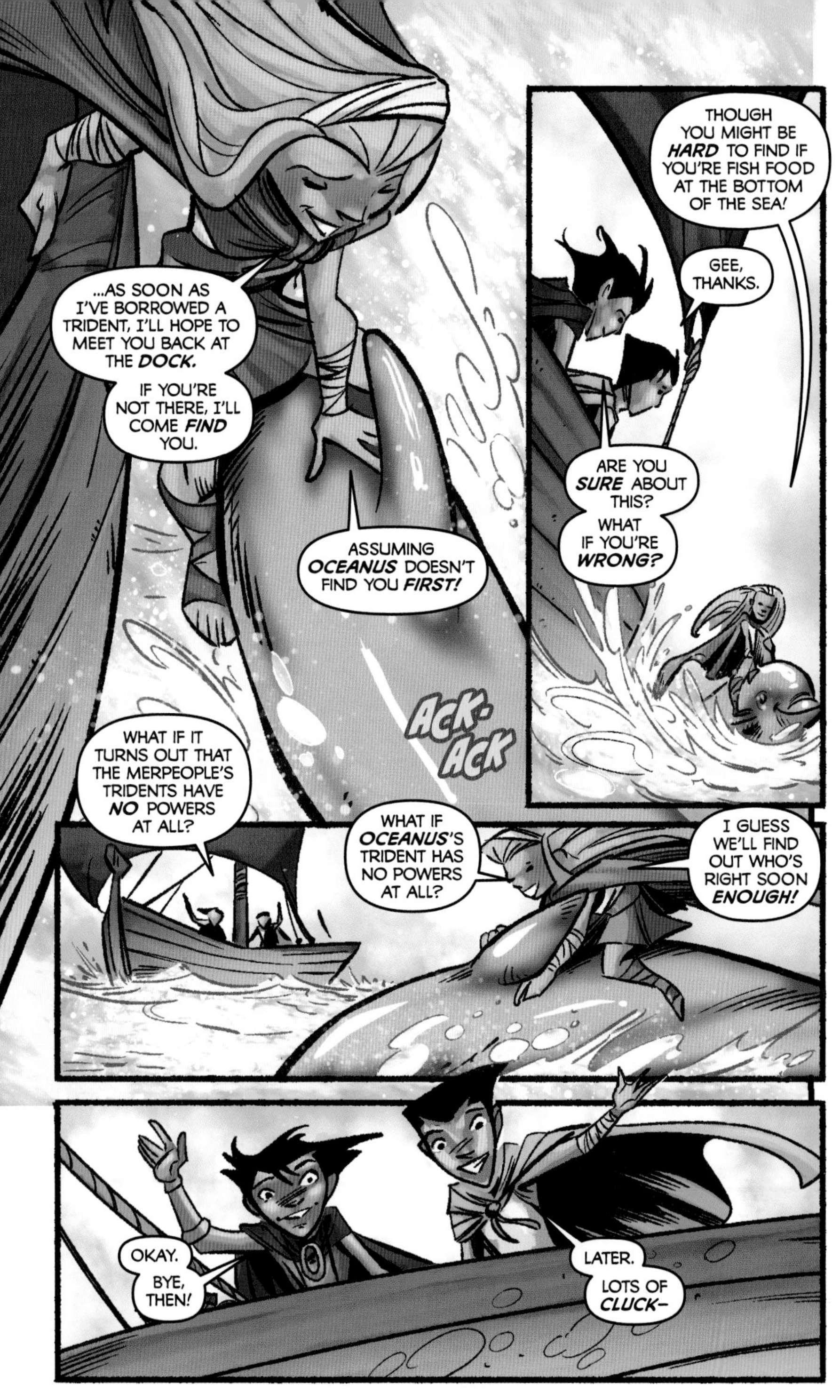
...AS SOON AS I'VE BORROWED A TRIDENT, I'LL HOPE TO MEET YOU BACK AT THE DOCK.
IF YOU'RE NOT THERE, I'LL COME FIND YOU.
ASSUMING OCEANUS DOESN'T FIND YOU FIRST!
THOUGH YOU MIGHT BE HARD TO FIND IF YOU'RE FISH FOOD AT THE BOTTOM OF THE SEA!
GEE, THANKS.
ARE YOU SURE ABOUT THIS?
WHAT IF YOU'RE WRONG?
ACK-ACK
WHAT IF IT TURNS OUT THAT THE MERPEOPLE'S TRIDENTS HAVE NO POWERS AT ALL?
WHAT IF OCEANUS'S TRIDENT HAS NO POWERS AT ALL?
I GUESS WE'LL FIND OUT WHO'S RIGHT SOON ENOUGH!
OKAY.
BYE, THEN!
LATER.
LOTS OF CLUCK–

I MEAN LUCK!
YOU SAW THAT, RIGHT?
WHOA.
WHEEEEEE!
FIRST THE SEA SERPENTS.
THEN THE MERPEOPLE.
AND NOW THE DOLPHIN!
ACK-ACK-ACK
WOOOSH!

POSEIDON, FOR SOMEONE SO SCARED OF THE *SEA...*
...YOU HAVE AN ODD EFFECT ON ITS *CREATURES!*
WELL, *I'M* THINKING ABOUT HOW ALL THESE CREATURES ARE SURVIVING THE BOILING SEA– JUST LIKE *WE* ARE!

COULD BE COLD POCKETS FROM DEEP DOWN, LIKE THE *FISHERMAN* SAID.
AND IT *COULD* BE THAT SOME OF THEM ARE PROTECTED BY MAGIC, LIKE MAYBE *WE* ARE.

SAY, WHAT DID YOU *SEE* WHEN THOSE SIRENS CALLED TO US?
YOU FIRST!
WHAT DID *YOU* SEE?

NOTHING.
IT'S *DUMB.*
LET'S JUST *GO.*
HE LOOKS *SORRY* THAT HE BROUGHT UP THE SUBJECT!

KRAK-KOOM!
YEOW!
HEY, YOU'RE AWFULLY JUMPY.
THAT'S JUST THUNDER.
IT'S NOT THUNDER I'M WORRIED ABOUT–IT'S THE LIGHTNING.
REMEMBER THAT FIRST DAY WE MET, I TOLD YOU GUYS HOW LIGHTNING ALWAYS MANAGES TO STRIKE ME?
THAT WAS REAL.
BUT YOU CONTROL A THUNDERBOLT!
WHY SHOULD IT–
OWWW!
YOU ARE THE ONE!
KRAKA-DOOOM!

I SEE WHAT YOU MEAN!
CAN'T YOU USE YOUR BOLT TO FIGHT BACK?
OWWW...
FIGHT... BACK...?
BZZZZT
BRZAP
KRK
KRK
KRK
LARGE, BOLT!
LARGE!
KRAKA-
-DOOOM!
KRA*KLE

KRA*KLE
KRA*KLE
KRA*K
KRA*K
KRA*K
YOU SHOW 'EM WHO'S *BOSS,* BOLT!
STINKER
KRA-KOOOM!
EEEEP!
UNNGH!

KRK
KRK
KRK
THANKS, BOLT! SMALL!
KRK
WOW!
ZEUS, YOU TOOK ON A LIGHTNING STORM. AND WON!
THAT WAS PRETTY GREAT, WASN'T IT?
I–
WAIT– WHAT'S WRONG WITH YOUR AMULET?
HUH?
OH. OKAY.
I THINK CHIP IS TELLING US WE'RE HERE!
NKER

SO WHERE'S *OCEANUS?*
UMMM... I THINK *HE'S* HERE *TOO!*
SPLOOOSSH
ZEUS'S PERFORMANCE WITH THE LIGHTNING WORKED LIKE A *BEACON*...

YAHHHHH!
SWOOOSH
...AND NOW OCEANUS IS *TOO* CLOSE FOR COMFORT!
HANG *ON!*
I'M HANGING! I'M *HANGING!*
ZEUS STILL BELIEVES LIGHTNING AND WATER DON'T MIX...
...AND HE ISN'T REALLY READY TO *TEST* HIS THEORY!
BOLT, *FLY* TO THE CLOSEST ISLAND!
WHIPP!
PRIZZT
WHOOOSH

CHAPTER SIX:
IN HOT WATER
SPLOOOSH
BLUB!
THE WATER MAY NOT *FEEL* AS HOT AS IT LOOKS...
...BUT ZEUS KNOWS HE IS IN HOT WATER IN *MORE* WAYS THAN ONE!

ZEUS!
ZEUS, WHERE ARE YOU?
GASP!
=WHEEZE=
KOFF KOFF
PLOOSH!

HERE I AM!
AND I SEE **YOU** DIDN'T **MELT,** AFTER ALL!
YEAH, WELL...
I COULD'VE **DROWNED,** THOUGH!
DID **OCEANUS** JUST THROW US?
I THINK SO.
MAYBE MY **LIGHTNING** STUNT WOKE HIM UP...
...IN A REALLY BAD MOOD!
SPLISH
THEN LET'S GET TO **LAND.**
THIS BOAT NEEDS **REPAIRS.**
YEAH.
AND I HAVE TO FIND **BOLT.**
WHAT ARE YOU DOING?
SPLASH
THIS WATER'S TOO ROUGH.
WE'RE GOING **NOWHERE** FAST.

WOW!
FWOOOSH!
I'M GIVING THINGS A LITTLE PUSH!
IS THE WATER IN ZEUS'S EARS CAUSING THAT CLACKING NOISE?
CLAK CLAK CLAK CLAK
I THOUGHT YOU SAID YOU COULDN'T SWIM!
GUESS I WAS WRONG!
LIKE THAT MELTING THING.
MY LAST MEMORY BEFORE BEING SWALLOWED...
...WAS CRONUS SAYING I WOULD MELT IF I WERE DROPPED INTO THE SEA!

UM, ZEUS, D'YOU THINK THAT, BESIDES CLAWED HANDS, OCEANUS HAS LOTS OF MUSCLES?
AND MAYBE A LONG BEARD?
HOW WOULD I KNOW?
UNLESS HE WAS ONE OF THOSE TITANS IN THE FOREST THE OTHER NIGHT...
...I'VE NEVER SEEN HIM!
CLAK CLAK CLAK CLAK
COULD HE HAVE HORNS ON TOP OF HIS HEAD?
HORNS THAT LOOK LIKE CRAB CLAWS?
HA-HA-HA!
HORNS "LIKE CRAB CLAWS?"

CLAK CLAK CLAK
CLAK
WHAT'S SO FUNNY ABOUT CRAB CLAW HORNS?
OCEANUS?
THAT'S MY NAME.
DON'T WEAR IT OUT.
UH, RIGHT.
GOOD ADVICE.
TAKE THE ADVICE, ZEUS!
TAKE THE ADVICE!

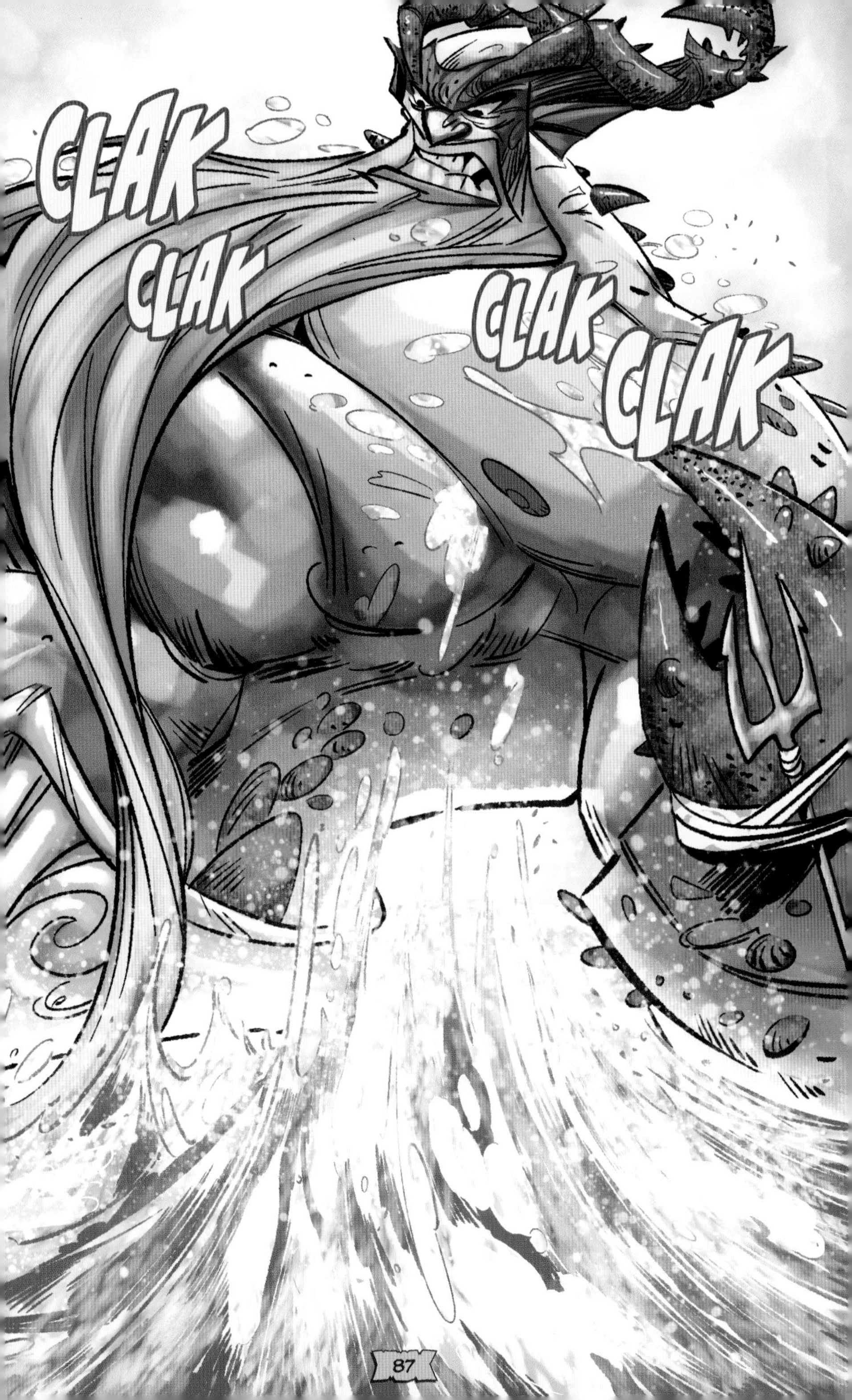
CLAK
CLAK
CLAK
CLAK

WELL?
STATE YOUR BUSINESS!
CLAK
CLAK
CLAK
CLAK
ALL RIGHT.
YOU TELL HIM, POSEIDON...
...POSEIDON?
THAT COWARD! IS HE HIDING UNDER THE BOAT?
IF ZEUS CAN GET TO THE ISLAND AND FIND BOLT, AT LEAST HE'LL HAVE A WEAPON!
WELL?
PYTHIA SENT US.
SHE'S THIS ORACLE AT DELPHI.
AND ACCORDING TO HER PROPHECY, I'M SUPPOSED TO FIND A MAGICAL TRIDENT!

I THOUGHT IF YOU'D LET ME BORROW *YOURS,* MAYBE I COULD USE IT TO *CALM* THE SEA, THEN–
WHAT?!
HOW *DARE* YOU?
I MADE THESE SEAS *FURIOUS*...
...AND FURIOUS THEY WILL *STAY!*
SKRRRAKK!
SPLASSH!
BUT... *WHY?*

BECAUSE I HAVE DECREED IT!
THAT'S NOT A REASON!
KA-RUMMPPH!
YOU OKAY?
SPLOOOSH!
YEAH. THANKS!
ARRRGH!

CLAK CLAK
I'VE SEEN IT, ZEUS—THE TRIDENT!
CLAK CLAK
IT'S ALL GOLD AND GLITTERY!
WAY MORE MAGNIFICENT THAN THAT MERPERSON'S TRIDENT!
HE'S GOT IT STRAPPED TO HIS CLAW LIKE A SWORD!
BEHIND YOU—WATCH OUT!
GIVE ME THAT TRIDENT, YOU OVERGROWN SEA BUG!
IT'S MINE!
OVERGROWN SEA BUG, AM I?
SMAKKK!
NASTY BUG!
NO MANNERS!

NOW ZEUS GETS IT.
NYAH, NYAH! MISSED ME!
YOU DON'T DESERVE THAT TRIDENT, CRABHEAD!
POSEIDON IS TRYING TO GOAD OCEANUS INTO USING THE TRIDENT SO THAT THEY CAN GRAB IT!
HEY, FISHBREATH!
YOUR TRIDENT IS FOOL'S GOLD, JUST LIKE YOU!
YOU'VE BEEN USING IT FOR EVIL INSTEAD OF GOOD!
NO POWERS AT ALL!
A TOTAL FAKE—JUST LIKE YOU!
FAKE, YOU SAY?
I'LL SHOW YOU HOW NOT FAKE IT IS!

HA-HA-HA-HA!
SKROOOM!
HERE WE GO!
UH-OH!
GLUB!

CHAPTER SEVEN:
BOLT OF CONFIDENCE
THAT WENT WELL.
THEY FOUND OCEANUS, GOT HIM TO UNSHEATHE THE TRIDENT...
...AND ZEUS MADE IT TO THE ISLAND TO FIND *BOLT.*
...UNNHHH...
NOW ZEUS HURTS IN PLACES HE DIDN'T KNOW HE HAD.
AND HE'S DISCOVERED THAT HE REALLY *HATES* HAVING *SAND* UP HIS NOSE!

TAKE THAT!
OW!
THUNDERATION! I CAN'T SEE MUCH OF ANYTHING THROUGH THE WATER IN MY EYES!
SPLASSH!
I NEED TO GET BACK OUT THERE TO HELP.
SIGH SOME HERO IN TRAINING I AM.
A TRUE HERO WOULD BE SIDE BY SIDE WITH POSEIDON RIGHT NOW.
P.U.
"STINKER" IS A PERFECT NAME FOR THIS BOAT, RIGHT NOW!

OKAY, STINKER!
STINKER
LET'S SEE HOW SEAWORTHY YOU STILL...
...ARE.
SIGH
INKER
SCRAPE
UNGHH
SO MUCH FOR THAT IDEA.
I NEED TO FIND SOMETHING TO MAKE SAILS OUT OF–AND SOMETHING TO PLUG THAT HOLE!

PZZZZT★
BOLT!
IS THAT YOU?
PZMMMT★
PZZZZZZT★
HEY– SETTLE DOWN!
I'M HERE!
HEY, WHAT GIVES? THIS IS EASY!
SLIPPP!
PZZZZT★
BRZZAPP
ZZZZZT!
WHY DIDN'T YOU GET LOOSE ON YOUR OWN?
ZZZZZZT!
IS THIS LIKE THE CONE-STONE IN PYTHIA'S TEMPLE?
MAYBE SOME KINDS OF ROCK ARE THUNDERBOLT TRAPS?
HA-HA! HAPPY TO SEE ME, EH?
OKAY– SMALL!
KRK★
KRK
KRK★
ZZZZZZIP!
ATTABOY!
NOW WE GOTTA PATCH A BOAT!

CHAPTER EIGHT:
SEA, WHIRLED
THIS TRIDENT IS *MINE!*
GLURRP!
SHOOOOSH

HOPE YOU'RE OUT FOR A LONG TIME AND TAKE A NICE NAP...
...UNTIL WE CAN GET FAR AWAY WITH MY TRIDENT.
BUT I NEED TO TAKE THE SCENIC ROUTE BACK.
THIS PLACE IS AMAZING!

THUDD
THUDD
THUDD
WAIT– THAT *CAN'T* BE!
THUDD
THUDD
HADES, IS THAT *YOU?*
POSEIDON!
HEY! SO GLAD YOU *FOUND* ME!
CRONUS ORDERED OCEANUS TO *IMPRISON* ME HERE!
TAKE A BIG *BREATH*...

...I'M GETTING YOU OUT!
KA-RAKKK!
POPP!
LET'S GET YOU BACK UP TO-
HUH? WHAT IS IT?
WOW! I WAS SO FOCUSED ON FIGHTING AND TRAPPING OCEANUS, I DIDN'T EVEN SEE IT!
THAT'S WHAT'S CAUSING THE SEA TO BOIL...

...AND I'VE GOT TO STOP IT!
SWOOOOP
KA-ROOMM!
IT'S NOT ENOUGH!

THAT'S IT!
BA-LOOOM
WITH *YOU* AND ME TOGETHER...
...WE'VE *GOT* THIS!
FSSSSSS
BLUMMBBLE
YES! I BEAT HIM!
POSEIDON! THANK GODS!
GASP!
HEY.
WHEEZE!
SPLASSH!

COMING ABOARD!
ZOOOOM
WHOA! NICE TRICK!
ZEUS, MEET HADES!
I REMEMBER YOU.
FREED US FROM CRONUS'S BELLY, RIGHT?
THANKS FOR NOTHING!
HEY! WHAT'S THAT SUPPOSED TO MEAN?
IT MEANS I LIKED IT IN THE BELLY.
IT WAS BETTER THAN BEING HELD UNDERSEA.
IT'S COLD DOWN THERE!
THE ONLY WARM MOMENT WAS WHEN WE PLUGGED THE VOLCANO!
WAIT, WHAT? VOLCANO?
AND THE SEA HAS BEEN BOILING, BUT YOU'RE COLD?
SHORT VERSION: I KNOCKED OUT OCEANUS.
TRAPPED HIM.
PLUGGED THE VOLCANO THAT WAS CAUSING THE SEA TO BOIL!
IT LOOKS LIKE THE TRIDENT IS IN THE RIGHT HANDS.

OCEANUS WON'T BE TRAPPED FOR LONG.
WE SHOULD SCRAM—AND QUICKLY!
HE'LL COME AFTER THE TRIDENT. AND US.
WE NEED TO IMPRISON HIM SOMEHOW WHILE WE HAVE THE UPPER HAND.
NO WAY!
ARE YOU BONKERS?
HE'S TOO BIG TO FIT ON THE BOAT.
CLAK CLAK CLAK
BESIDES, ONE FLIP OF HIS TAIL OR SLICE FROM HIS CLAW...
THEN WHAT DO YOU GUYS SUGGEST?
NO, THAT WON'T WORK. WE–
OH NO...
CLAK CLAK CLAK CLAK
RUN!

CHAPTER NINE:
TITAN TRANSPORT
CLAK
CLAK
CLAK
CLAK
THERE IS NO ESCAPE FROM ME, FOOLISH CHILDREN!
JUMP ON! HURRY!
TOLD YOU WE SHOULD SCRAM!
TOLD YOU WE SHOULD IMPRISON HIM!
KRRUNNCH!
SWOOOOSH

PZZZT!
YOU'RE *RIGHT!* WE HAVE TO *DEAL* WITH HIM!
OH BOY!
NO! TURN AWAY! *TURN AWAY!*

BOLT, *HOVER!*
WHAT'S A *"BOLT"?*
SPLASH

IN THIS MOMENT, ZEUS UNDERSTANDS POSEIDON'S NOT NEEDING TO BREATHE UNDERWATER...

...POSEIDON'S NEW STRENGTH AND SWIMMING ABILITY, FISH GIVING THEMSELVES UP WHENEVER HE'S HUNGRY.

WA-HOOO! IS THIS THE *COOLEST,* OR WHAT?

THE WAY SEA SERPENTS, MERPEOPLE, AND THAT DOLPHIN ALL STARE AT HIM.

THE CREATURES OF THE SEA RECOGNIZE *POSEIDON* AS THEIR *LEADER.*

THE TRIDENT REALLY WAS INTENDED FOR HIM. POSEIDON'S HANDS ARE THE *RIGHT* HANDS!

HE'S TURNING TAIL...
...MAKING A BREAK FOR IT!
YOU INSPIRED ME. WATCH!
LONG!
SPLASH!
DON'T WORRY– I HAVE AN IDEA!
I'M GOING FISHING.
I'LL SNAG THAT TITAN IN NO TIME!
FWOOOSH

THAT'S AMAZING!
ARRRGH!
HA-HA! I'VE SNAGGED HIM!
NOW WHAT?
AND YOUR TAIL IS SO COOL!
NOW WE REEL HIM IN!
GOTCHA!
WHOA!
YIPE!
CLAK
CLAK
RELEASE ME AT ONCE!
CLAK
CLAK
SPLOOOSH

RELEASE YOU?!
NOT GONNA HAPPEN!
NOPE!
NOPE!
CLAK CLAK CLAK
NOPE!
YOU'RE OUR PRISONER NOW!
HA! I DON'T THINK THIS IS GOING TO HELP YOU, SNACKBOY–
HA-HA-HA! THAT TOY?
YOU'RE RIGHT!
BUT I THINK MY THUNDERBOLT COULD HELP JOLT YOUR HELPFULNESS!
PZZZT
BR-ZAP-PP!
YEOWW!
KRA★KLE
YUP. THAT ONE.

ONWARD! TAKE US TO, UM, LAND.
I'LL DIRECT YOU BACK TO THE DOCK WE STARTED FROM.
HA-HA! YOU WANT ME TO GIVE YOU A RIDE?
BE GLAD TO...
...BUT FIRST, YOU'LL HAVE TO FREE ME FROM THIS NET SO I CAN SWIM PROPERLY!
NO WAY!
HOW DUMB DO YOU THINK WE ARE?
WELL, ON A SCALE OF DUMBNESS FROM ONE TO TEN, I'D SAY–
GET MOVING!
OWW!
ZEUS CAN HARDLY BELIEVE THAT OCEANUS OBEYS!
BUT POSEIDON LEARNS QUICKLY HOW TO USE HIS TRIDENT, SO THE TITAN DOESN'T HAVE MUCH CHOICE.

WHAT'LL WE DO WITH HIM AFTER WE'RE BACK IN GREECE?
HE'LL BE A DANGER TO ALL OLYMPIANS IF WE LET HIM GO FREE.
HEH! YOU GOT THAT RIGHT!
WHACK!
STOP LISTENING!
WE HAVE TO KEEP HIM TIED UP IN THIS NET UNTIL WE CAN IMPRISON HIM.
WHERE WILL WE FIND A PRISON STRONG ENOUGH TO HOLD HIM?
HUH?
AKE-TIP ITAN-TIP O-TIP ARTARUS-TIP.
"TAKE TITAN TO TARTARUS." UHH...WHERE'S THAT?
NO CLUE!
HEY, LOOK!
SEEMS LIKE THAT'S THE ROUTE TO TARTARUS...
...AND THE DOCK IS ALONG THE WAY!

I DON'T SEE HERA!
I FIGURED SHE'D BE WAITING FOR US!
MAYBE I ATE HER ALREADY! YOU NEVER KNOW...
SHUT UP! JUST SHUT UP!
MAYBE KING CRONUS CAPTURED HER AGAIN?
I DIDN'T KNOW YOU CARED!
JUST BECAUSE I FIGHT WITH HER DOESN'T MEAN I WANT HER TO GET RECAPTURED.
ALL THREE OF US ARE OLYMPIANS, AFTER ALL.
I VOTE WE KEEP GOING.
WE CAN SWING BACK AND SEARCH FOR HERA LATER.
HE'S RIGHT.
WE HAVE TO LOCK OCEANUS UP FOR EVERYONE'S SAFETY...
...INCLUDING HERA'S!
I VOTE THAT YOU-
THAT "SHUT UP" THING?
WE MEANT IT!

WHERE ARE YOU TAKING ME?
THAT'S FOR US TO KNOW AND YOU TO...
...UH, NOT KNOW.
JUST MARCH!
JAB!
OWW! WATCH IT WITH THAT THING!
THEN PICK UP THE PACE!
YOU SURE ARE POPULAR HERE.
IT'S A TITAN, COME TO DESTROY US!
RUN!
HEY, LOOK WHO IT IS!
HELLO, KIND SIR!
WE'VE COMPLETED THE FIRST PART OF OUR QUEST!
I SEE THAT!
VERY BRAVE OF YOU!
WE STOPPED THE VOLCANO THAT CAUSED THE SEA TO BOIL!
BEFORE LONG, EVERYTHING SHOULD BE BACK TO NORMAL!
MANY THANKS, YOUNG MASTERS...

"...INDEED, THE GODS ARE GOOD."
WE HAVE ONE OF YOUR THREE MISSING FRIENDS AND THE TRIDENT NOW.
SO WHAT WAS THE BIG SECRET HERA WAS GOING TO TELL ME, ONCE WE GOT IT?
I PROMISED NOT TO SAY.
YOU'LL HAVE TO ASK HER...
...IF WE EVER SEE HER AGAIN.
HUSH! THINGS ARE MOVING UP THERE.
HE'S RIGHT.
WHAT WAS THAT–A CRONY?
UNFORTUNATELY NOT.
CRONIES WEAR ARMOR. I LIKE CRONIES.
THEN WHAT?
MAYBE WE SHOULD HIDE AND–

CHAPTER TEN:
THE ANDROPHAGOI
YAAAAH!
ZEUS RECALLS KING CRONUS, IN HIS FOREST MEETING OF TITANS, PLANNING TO *UNLEASH* THE CREATURES OF CHAOS.
PYTHIA MENTIONED THEM IN HER *PROPHECY.*
CRONUS HAS LET LOOSE THE FIRST *CREATURES OF CHAOS!*
WE'RE *DOOMED!*
DIDN'T SHE SAY THE *TRIDENT* COULD *DEFEAT* THEM?

THOSE ARE ANDROPHAGOI COMING AT US!
THEY'RE MONSTERS!
HAVE YOU LOOKED AT YOURSELF?
SO ARE YOU!

DON'T YOU GET IT?
THEY'RE MAN-EATERS!
THEY'LL EAT US ALIVE! INCLUDING ME!

"IT'S AN AMBUSH!"
YAAAAAAH!!

SPREAD OUT AND CLIMB!
ZEUS WONDERS IF BOLT AND POSEIDON'S TRIDENT WILL BE A MATCH AGAINST THIS ARMY OF MONSTERS.
NO TIME LIKE THE PRESENT TO FIND OUT!
WE CAN PICK THEM OFF ONE BY ONE FROM HIGH IN THE TREES!
TWEEEEEET
THOK!

WHAT ABOUT ME?
THOK! TWEEEEEET
THOK! TWEEEEEET
PZZZT!
HIDE SOMEWHERE!
BUT DON'T YOU DARE TRY TO ESCAPE!
BOLT–LARGE!
PZZZT!
AFTER THEM!
THE ANDROPHAGOI, I MEAN!
KRA•KLE

SWOOOSH
PZZZZT
KRA-KLE
YAAAH!
TAKE THAT!
HUH? NOW THAT'S INTERESTING!
POP!
POP!
POP!
ZEUS– CHECK IT OUT!
POP!
POP!
THEY SEEM TO BE UNDER SOME KIND OF ENCHANTMENT!
POP!
FOR YOU, MAYBE!
MY THUNDERBOLT JUST FRIES THEM!
POP!
THAT GIVES ME AN IDEA!
POP!
POP!

YOU'VE GOT A PLAN?
TRUST ME ON THIS.
THROW YOUR TRIDENT TOWARD THE FOREST— HARD!
I JUST HOPE IT WORKS!
BOLT, GUIDE THE TRIDENT!
POP THEM...
BZZZT*
WHOOOOSH!
...POP THEM ALL!
POP!

PZZZZT*
KRA*KLE
POP!
POP!
SWOOOOSH
POP!
POP!
YAAAAAH!
POP!

PZZZZT*
KRA*KLE
POP!
SWIIISSSSSSH
POP!
YAAAAAH!
POP!

YAAAAAAH!
UH-OH.

WHOA!
GOOD THING THEY DON'T HAVE SAWS!
THWAKK!
THWAKK!
THWAKK!
YAAAH!
NO– BACK OFF!
YAAAH!
FLUMP
BUT THE ANDROPHAGOI DO HAVE LEGS!
HERE, BOLT!
COME HERE, BOY!
TWEEEEET!

"BOLT!"
PZZZZT*
KRA*KLE
POP!
POP!
SWOOOOSH
BOLT IS TOO FAR AWAY. ZEUS REALIZES THAT HE IS ON HIS *OWN!*
YAAAAAH!
YOU SURE HAVE A *LIMITED* VOCABULARY!
CHOMP! CHOMP!
WHY DOES *EVERY* CREATURE I MEET WANT TO *EAT* ME?
CHOMP!
GET OFF!
WHUMP
WHUMP
OH BOY.
SNAP!

HEH! THAT WASN'T SO BAD!
WHUMMP!
THUMMP!
SPOKE TOO SOON!
THOK!
THWIPP!
THWIPP!
THOK!
OH, NONONO!
YAAAAAH!
YAAAAAH!

BOLT!
SWOOOSH
BZZZT
POP!
ABOUT TIME YOU GOT HERE.
ZZIIIP
BZZZT
IT ALMOST CHOMPED ME!
I'M SORRY. THAT WASN'T FAIR.
I KNOW YOU WERE BUSY.
WAIT–BOLT, YOU GOT ALL OF THEM?
GREAT WORK!
GREAT TEAMWORK!
BZZZT

ZZZZIP!
PZZZT
YOU'RE BETTER THAN ANY OL' GOLDEN TRIDENT.
I'LL MISS YOU WHEN YOU GO BACK TO THAT GOOSE GUY!
SO WE'VE WON?
THEY'RE GONE?
WAIT– WHERE'S OCEANUS?
HERE.
I'M JUST HERE.
SIGH

WE SAVED YOUR LIFE.
BZZZZZT
SNIPP
SNIPP
YOU SHOULD BE GRATEFUL!
SLICE!
CUT MY ARMS FREE WHILE YOU'RE AT IT.
I PROMISE I WON'T TRY TO ESCAPE.
DON'T BELIEVE HIM!
HE'S CROSSING HIS CLAWS!
SWEAR, OCEANUS.
SWEAR ON THE TRIDENT!
FINE.
I SWEAR I WON'T ESCAPE.

ANDROPHAGOI.
HE SENT ACTUAL CREATURES OF CHAOS!
YEAH, YOU'VE BEEN FOLLOWING HIS ORDERS!
WE KNEW THAT A LONG TIME AGO!
IT TOOK AN ARMY OF MAN-EATING MONSTERS TO CLUE YOU IN?
I NEVER THOUGHT I'D SAY THIS ABOUT ANOTHER TITAN...
...BUT IT SEEMS LIKE CRONUS CAN'T BE TRUSTED.
LIKE KEEPING ME CAPTIVE!!
I HAD MY REASONS.
CRONUS IS MY KING. I OWE HIM ALLEGIANCE.
BESIDES, HE TOLD ME YOU WERE PLOTTING TO OVERTHROW HIM.
ME...?

I DON'T KNOW HOW TO OVERTHROW ANYBODY!
I SPENT MY ENTIRE LIFE IN CRONUS'S STOMACH!
IT WASN'T OUR FAULT THAT CRONUS SWALLOWED US WHOLE!
WE NEVER EVEN KNEW HIM...
...WE WERE LITTLE KIDS AT THE TIME!
TAKK!
CAREFUL!
IF YOU DROP MY TRIDENT, I'LL–

YOU'LL DO **NOTHING!**
THIS TRIDENT IS **NOT YOURS!**
IT NEVER WAS. IT'S **MINE.**
YOU **STOLE** IT!
I DID NOT!
CRONUS **GAVE** IT TO ME **YEARS** AGO!
IT WAS **NEVER** HIS TO GIVE AWAY.
WHEN THE SIRENS SANG TO US ON OUR JOURNEY, I SAW A **VISION** OF MYSELF...
...AS A **BABY**— PLAYING WITH THIS VERY **TRIDENT!**
AHA!
THAT EXPLAINS YOUR WEIRD GLANCES AT **POSEIDON!**
YOU KNEW **ALL ALONG** THAT THE TRIDENT WAS **HIS!**
YET YOU HAD THE **NERVE** TO THREATEN ME WHEN I ASKED TO **BORROW** IT!

DID CRONUS THREATEN TO TAKE BACK THE TRIDENT IF YOU DIDN'T IMPRISON ME?
SIGH
CLAK
CLAK
CLAK
CLAK
TO TELL THE TRUTH, CRONUS HAS ALWAYS BEEN SORT OF A BAD APPLE.
WHEN WE WERE YOUNG, HE'D LIE TO GET ME IN TROUBLE...
...JUST FOR FUN!
ALWAYS TELLING OUR PARENTS THAT I PINCHED HIM!
WAIT, WHAT?
YOUR PARENTS?
DOES THAT MEAN YOU'RE–
YUP, BROTHERS. CRONUS IS MY LITTLE BROTHER, TO BE EXACT.
MY SPOILED, BRATTY LITTLE BROTHER!
AND NOW THAT HE'S UNLEASHED THE CREATURES OF CHAOS...
...MORTALS AND GODS ALIKE...
...ARE ALL DOOMED!

CRONUS IS SCHEMING TO RULE OVER EVERYONE WHO SURVIVES...
...AND THE ONLY THREATS TO HIS PLAN ARE OLYMPIANS!
BUT WHY ARE THEY A THREAT?
HOW? SOME KIND OF MAGICAL POWERS?
YOU MEAN YOU DON'T KNOW?
BECAUSE OF THE PROPHECY!
WHAT PROPHECY?
"AN OLYMPIAN SHALL RISE UP AND LEAD OTHER OLYMPIANS TO DEFEAT CRONUS."
KRACKKK!
BUT–
WHAT NOW?
RUMMMBLE

CHAPTER ELEVEN:
THE ORACLE
CONGRATULATIONS!
THE TRIDENT IS NOW IN THE RIGHT HANDS!
PYTHIA!
YES!
FSSSSSSS

SEE? I KNEW IT WAS MINE!
IF USED WISELY, THAT TRIDENT WILL BRING UNTOLD POWER...
SHHHH! LET HER FINISH!
...AND GLORY...
...AND HONOR...
...TO THE TRUE GOD OF THE SEA!
STUPEFYING STARFISH!
I'M THE GOD OF THE SEA!

THAT EXPLAINS A LOT!
OCEANUS BEING AFRAID OF YOU WASN'T JUST BECAUSE OF THE TRIDENT.
IF YOU'RE GOD OF THE SEA, THEN OCEANUS IS BENEATH YOU IN RANK!
YOU'RE HIS MASTER!
YEAH. WOW!
YOU HAVE ALSO DEFEATED THE FIRST OF THE KING'S CREATURES OF CHAOS!
WELL DONE.
BUT YOUR QUESTS HAVE NOT YET ENDED.
WE THREE HAVE DONE PRETTY WELL SO FAR!
NEXT YOU MUST FIND THE HELM OF DARKNESS!
HUH?
THE WHAT OF WHO?

THE HELM OF DARKNESS RIGHTFULLY BELONGS TO THE ONE WHO IS LORD OF THE UNDERWORLD!
FIND IT– AND YOU WILL ALSO FIND MORE OF THE PERSONS YOU SEEK!
BUT BEWARE OF THE SECOND OF CRONUS'S CREATURES OF CHAOS!
FOR THEY ARE FAR, FAR MORE DANGEROUS THAN THE ANDROPHAGOI!

SO WHAT IS A HELM OF DARKNESS?
WHO'S THE LORD OF THE–
WAIT!
STOP!
RUMMMMBLE
SHE'S GONE.
AGAIN.
MORE CREATURES OF CHAOS?
I DO NOT LIKE THE SOUND OF THAT.
WHAT DO YOU THINK OF ALL THIS, OCEANUS?
DO YOU KNOW ANYTHING ABOUT THESE NEXT CREATURES OF CHAOS?
OCEANUS?
OH NO– HE ESCAPED!
ALL OUR ATTENTION WAS ON THE ORACLE!
SO MUCH FOR HIS PROMISE!

MAYBE NO TITAN CAN BE TRUSTED!
I CAN'T SPOT HIM ANYWHERE!
WHERE DOES A TITAN THAT BIG HIDE, ANYWAY?
NO NEED TO PANIC.
CHIP SEEMS TO BE ABLE TO GIVE US DIRECTIONS TO ANYONE ANYWHERE IN THE WORLD!
SO, CHIP—CAN YOU SHOW US WHERE OCEANUS IS?
OPE-NIP!
"NOPE"...? WHAT? YOU CAN'T?
OR YOU WON'T?
ONE-GIP!
SO..."NOT HERE"?
OKAY, THEN... HERA!
SHOW US THE WAY TO HERA!
OPE-NIP!

"NOPE" AGAIN? WHAT'S WRONG WITH IT?
IS THIS THING BROKEN?
OPE-NIP! OPE-NIP!
WHA-? "NOPE" AGAIN?!
YOU'RE USELESS!
NO!
C'MON, HADES...
...STOP BEING SUCH A HOTHEAD!
SWOOOSH
WE NEED CHIP.
SORRY! BUT WHAT DO WE DO NOW?
I HAVE ANOTHER IDEA.
WHIPP
PZZZZT

OKAY, BOLT– LET'S SEE HOW GOOD A HUNTER YOU ARE!
GO GET OCEANUS!
KRA-KLE
BR-ZZAP
WHOOOOSH
YOUR BOLT IS BROKEN, TOO?
SWIPPP!
ZAP
NO. I THINK IT MEANS THAT OCEANUS IS NOWHERE IN THE WORLD!
HOW IS THAT EVEN POSSIBLE?
ASKS THE GUY WHO LIVED IN A TITAN'S BELLY ALL HIS LIFE?
POINT TAKEN.
DO YOU THINK OCEANUS IS OFF TELLING KING CRONUS WHAT PYTHIA SAID?
I HOPE NOT.
BUT THERE'S NO REASON TO GO TO TARTARUS NOW.
LET'S HEAD TO THE UNDERWORLD INSTEAD–
FAST...

...BEFORE THOSE HALF-GIANT CRONIES CAN BEAT US THERE.
IF THAT "HELM OF DARKNESS" THING BELONGS TO THE LORD OF THE UNDERWORLD, THAT'S PROBABLY WHERE WE'LL FIND IT!
FUNNY... IT'S STILL POINTING THE SAME WAY IT DID BEFORE.
THUMP
THUMP
THUMP
EITHER IT'S BROKEN, LIKE I SAID...
COULD BE!
...OR TARTARUS IS NEAR THE UNDERWORLD!
ALL I KNOW FOR SURE IS THAT WE SHOULD HEAD FOR THE RIVER!
LOOKS GLOOMY.
AND I BET IT SMELLS BAD TOO!
SOUNDS PERFECT!

OH YEAH....
HADES LIKES GLOOMY AND STINKY STUFF LIKE THE INSIDE OF THE KING'S BELLY.
HUH?
WHAT A WEIRDO, ZEUS DECIDES.
ARE THE OTHER OLYMPIANS THAT ZEUS HASN'T MET JUST AS WEIRD?
CERTAINLY POSEIDON IS ALL RIGHT–A GREAT OLYMPIAN WITH GREAT POWER!
AND IF ALL THESE OLYMPIANS ARE GODS, THAT WOULD MAKE HERA A GODDESS!
BUT OF WHAT? THE GODDESS OF BEING ANNOYING?
SHE CAN BE A PAIN AT TIMES, BUT ZEUS LIKES HAVING HER AROUND.
BUT WHY DIDN'T SHE WAIT FOR THEM LIKE SHE'D SAID SHE WOULD?

AND WHY CAN'T THE ORACLE EVER GIVE THEM A STRAIGHT ANSWER?
ARE ALL ORACLES LIKE THAT, OR JUST PYTHIA?
MAYBE THIS NEW QUEST WILL LEAD ZEUS TO THOSE ANSWERS...
FOLLOW ME, GUYS!
IT'S TIME TO FACE ANOTHER ADVENTURE TOGETHER!
...ABOUT HERA, ABOUT THE OTHER OLYMPIANS...
...EVEN ABOUT THAT GOOSE GUY WHO WILL SOMEDAY INHERIT BOLT.